Why do we play

GW01239162

A little book of verse for the bewildered lady golfer.

Contents

Ballad of the Beginner

I step up to the tee and address the ball

And politely ask it to go straight, that's all

Or failing that just leave the tee

That would be enough for me

But the ball's so small and so far away

I don't think it can hear a word that I say.

My practice swing is perfect, no trouble at all

This game would be a lot easier without the ball.

I take a deep breath, take another swing

And don't even make contact with the stupid thing.

My other half starts to give me hints and tips

About what to do with my head and my hips,

I'll tell him what to do with his wedge in a minute.

This game tests your patience right to the limit.

Somehow or other I get near to the green

But I've taken so many shots it's quite obscene.

I flap at the ball with a fly swatting action

And manage to move it just a fraction.

'Don't break your wrists,' says he, 'that you must never do.'

I tell him that I wasn't planning to, mind you,

Casualty might not be a bad place to end up

At least it would get me out of the Smitten Cup.*

I'm in the woods on the 8th now, sobbing bitterly

That's the third time in a row I've hit that tree

At this rate I'll be stuck out here all night

And the greenkeepers are in for a fright

When they find me knee deep in leaves, surrounded by conkers

Slowly going stark raving bonkers.

Eventually I get near the 18th green, not bad going

Although I started out in summer and now it's snowing.

There are only two bunkers at Epsom and guess what

I land in one with my 150th shot

I manage to get out first time, what luck!

But the ball flies into the other bunker, oh... dear

I'll be stuck here forever going from one to the other,

And my children will have to grow up without a mother.

It's finally over and God, I need a drink

The 19th hole's the one for me, I think.

'What did you go round in asks?' my other half.

What's he doing, having a laugh?

'I went round in a huff,' is all I'm prepared to say.

I'm not telling him my score, no bloody way.

'Do you want to give up?' he says, sensing my sorrow,

'Not likely', I reply, 'I'm going out again tomorrow!'

* Formerly a competition strictly for married couples but now fully inclusive and open to partners of any persuasion or orientation. (see 'Playing with your Partner' for more details)

Learning

You've been playing for a while, you've got the bug

It's all going really well, you're feeling quite smug.

OK so you don't always hit the ball that precisely

But your handicap has started to come down nicely,

And all things being equal, you're now fairly sure

You'll come down a shot or two, maybe even more.

Yes, you've got this game well under control

A single figure handicap, that's your goal!

But in golf it's always fatal to plan ahead,

Well, not fatal as such, you're not likely to drop dead.

No, it's far worse than that, in its own way,

You're going to suddenly forget how to play.

Oh no, what's gone wrong? You're at a complete loss

But it's just the game of golf showing you who's boss.

It does this to everyone, puts us all to the test

Even the tour Professionals and they're the very best,

Plus they've got coaches and physios and psychologists

And all sorts of other highly trained ologists.

They should be able to play with their eyes shut

But even they can shank a shot, duff a putt

And there's poor you, new to golf, and all on your own

No wonder your game looks like its currently on loan

From a one-armed crazy golfer with a blindfold on,

But don't worry, it's just a phase, it'll soon be gone.

So if your game has suddenly gone chronic,

And someone says, (presumably trying to be ironic)

'Just go out and enjoy yourself, that's the main thing.'

Instead of head butting them until their ears ring

Just picture Ernie Els six putting at the Masters

And remember that we all have our little disasters.

So here's another lesson you need to learn,

Just follow the example of good old Ern

Who had a short putt and thought he could read it,

Keep a sense of humour. You're going to need it.

Playing with your Partner

For the purpose of this verse your partner will be

Someone who identifies as a he

Because keeping gender equality in mind

I know I can't make assumptions of any kind.

Your partner may be a he, she or it

Or not exactly sure where they fit.

They could be a transvestite in all his/ her finery

Or someone who identifies as non-binary.

They may be transgender or perhaps they're bi

Or they could be someone who's willing to try

Anything really, which makes them a Q

(And in case you're wondering, Q who?

Not the guy in the Bond films who, by the way,

Once was straight but now is gay.)

Q is for questioning and by now you probably are too

Because it's so difficult to know what to say or do

When all the old rules no longer seem to apply

But there is one thing on which you can still rely,

Play golf with your partner and almost without fail,

Provided he identifies as a heterosexual male,

(If indeed such a term is still allowed)

Then he will almost certainly be endowed

With a superior knowledge of the game to you

And immediately start telling you what to do.

It begins on the first tee. He'll look at you askance

And then he'll try and change your stance,

Or assess how you're lined up and then he'll say,

'You'll go in the trees if you hit it that way.'

So in order to avoid any early altercations

You duly make the requested alterations,

But it feels all wrong now, you're ill at ease

And so you hit it straight into the trees.

It's not his fault, of course, you just didn't do

Exactly what he told you to.

You get on the fairway eventually

After your misadventures on the tee

And with club in hand, you're about to play

When he'll suck in his breath and then he'll say,

'I'd take a seven wood there if I were you.'

Now it's not as if you don't know what to do.

So with a smile that can best be described as frozen,

You say, 'I'm quite happy with the club I've chosen.'

It's not as if you haven't hit this shot before

But even so you're now all of a dither, you're not so sure,

Because he's sown little niggling seeds of doubt

So you reluctantly get your seven wood out

And hit a real stinker of a shot

But it's not his fault, of course it's not,

You just didn't hit the shot the way you should.

(Hardly surprising, with that bloody wood!)

By now you're starting to feel really on edge

So when for your next shot you choose a wedge

And again he does that sucking in breath thing,

You just ignore him and take your swing

And your head flies up, it's all such a mess,

And what does he say? I expect you can guess.

'That was always going to be the wrong club there.'

By now, of course, you're going completely spare.

But unfortunately there's more to come.

You're standing on the green now, looking glum

While he's showing you the borrow and the line,

'Just hit it over there and you'll be fine.'

But you're really not sure that you agree,

He's showing you a line you just can't see,

Although to be honest you no longer have a clue

What on earth it is you're supposed to do.

You take the putt, not the best you've ever seen

It not only misses the hole, it rolls off the green.

'You should have listened to what I said,' he tutts,

'I know what I'm talking about when it comes to putts.'

(Is there anything about this game he doesn't know?

Oh well, only another seventeen holes to go.)

Its finally over. You see the divorce court beckon

And then he says, 'Why is it, do you reckon,

That you played such rubbish golf today?'

He just doesn't get it, there's simply no way

That he's going to take any of the blame,

He was just showing you how to play the game.

Perhaps this all comes back to sexuality,

He's your average bloke with a bloke's mentality.

A bi-sexual wouldn't be so dogmatic

He'd be in two minds, a bit more pragmatic,

While a transvestite would probably be

Too busy fussing with all his/her finery

To worry about what club you took and where

And a transgender would neither know nor care,

Far too busy checking what was still there.

Now I'm not suggesting all men are the same.

When it comes to playing the couples game.

Your chap may be a real sweetie on the course

Totally supportive, ready to endorse

Every single shot you choose to play

(In which case are you sure he's not gay?)

But joking aside, the chances are

That if he's never likely to wear a bra

Or be in two minds or ready to surrender

Parts that can best be described as tender,

If he's a full male member, it's fair to say

He's probably going to tell you how to play.

So how to get round this, how to keep calm

When you're thinking divorce, gross bodily harm?

Well, if couples golf is really such a big ask

May I suggest gaffer tape, earplugs, a hip flask?

But if you find you're still at the end of your tether

You could abstain from conjugal golf altogether,

Although there is another option open to you,

Try playing with someone who's trans or bi or Q!

No Brainer

Golf really is a most infuriating game,

Everybody you talk to tells you the same,

It gives you glimpses of how you could play

Then just as quickly snatches them away.

So to solve this conundrum, off you go

And have some lessons with your club Pro.

He* looks at your game with a critical eye

Tells you what you're doing wrong and why

And gives you all sorts of helpful tips

About how to cure your putting yips

And your hook, your slice, your overswing

He's got a solution to everything.

And in the lesson it all makes perfect sense

Because you don't feel the slightest bit tense

Your swing's superb, the shots just flow

In the comforting presence of the Pro.

But when you get out on the course alone

Then alas, you once again become prone

To make all the mistakes you made before

And what's worse, you've added some more!

'Oh no,' you wail, 'this is tragic,

And in the lesson it worked like magic'.

So how best to ease your frustration

And avoid repeated humiliation?

Simple! Get a blow up of your Pro.

I can hear you thinking, hang on, wait a mo,

I like the guy, but not that much,

It's not as if I'm craving his touch

So if my desires are not insatiable

Why on earth would I need an inflatable?

And besides just think of all the chafing

You'd get from having a rubber plaything.

Steady on there! Don't get too carried away.

I wasn't trying to lead you astray,

By suggesting anything rude or obscene,

Perhaps I'd better explain what I mean.

Remember when the Pro gave you tuition

And everything just came to fruition?

Your putts, your chips, all sublime

Your swing working a treat every time.

And all because the Pro was there.

So why not take a blow up of him everywhere?

(When you play, I mean, not on the bus

That might cause a bit of a fuss)

But have him on the course in inflatable form

Then lesson standard golf will become the norm.

Because just the sight of him hovering around,

(Tethered securely, of course, to the ground)

Will give you all the confidence you need

To play immaculate golf, guaranteed.

So if you'd like an on-course trainer,

Go ahead, it's a complete no-brainer

Get an inflatable of your Pro,

All you have to do is blow.

* you may substitute 'she', 'they' or' it' for the word 'he.'

Winning Smile

You join a golf club and then after a little while

The lady captain waylays you with a winning smile

And asks a question, innocent so it seems,

But the answer to it should be, 'in your dreams,'

Because she's asking you to join the committee.

'Don't say no,' she says, 'that would be such a pity

Because you'd be ideal, somebody like you.'

(What she really means is anyone will do.)

At first you refuse but she won't leave it there

'Surely you've got a little time to spare,

And you can do what you want, take your pick.'

(Yes, they always get you with that old trick.)

It goes on like this til finally you say yes

Though what it all involves is anyone's guess.

At first, not much, you just lend a hand

But then your duties seem to expand

And after what only seems a little while

The lady Captain waylays you with a winning smile,

And in wheedling tones of which you've become wary

Says, 'I can see you as Treasurer or Secretary.'

Then of course you immediately start stalling,

'I can't add up. My admin skills are appalling.'

But all your objections are blithely brushed aside,

You don't know apparently until you've tried.

So you do either or both jobs after a fashion

Although you hate the adding up with a passion,

And then when you're feeling fairly sure

That you've done your bit and much, much more

And you're planning to step down in a little while,

The lady captain waylays you with a winning smile

'I'd like you to be my vice captain,' she simpers

And then ignoring your horrified whimpers,

Says you'd be ideal, it's a job you'd love.

(For the meaning of ideal please see above)

You say no to start with, like you always do

But people aren't exactly forming an orderly queue

To take on the honour of the captaincy role

So although it's something that was never your goal,

You say yes, because you're the only one,

Then before you know it, your year has begun.

And though you've only been in the job a few hours,

You suddenly seem to have developed special powers.

Hey presto! You're Wonder Woman, all knowing,

Able to answer every question going,

While also taking everything in your stride

Oh yes, and keeping everyone satisfied,

Even though what they want is never the same

But if they don't get it you're the one to blame.

And if you think all this sounds pretty bad

You also have to do it scantily clad!

(Only joking, it's not yet required of you

To actually wear the Wonder Woman outfit too.)

Now, it may be that after all this you still feel

That Captain is a job for which you'd be, 'ideal'.

In that case, go for it! Give it all you've got,

But if you're thinking, actually, no, I'd rather not,

When the lady captain waylays you with a winning smile,

Take my advice. Run a mile!

Magic Elixir

Let's face it, we're not all of us in the first flush

But some, I know, would like to keep this hush hush,

So to save our blushes, I'll put it delicately then,

A lot of us aren't likely to see ......ty again

(Insert the number with which you identify

Because when it comes to age it's OK to lie.)

But so what if we put eight, seven or six here?

Because we've discovered a magic elixir

That makes the whole thorny question of age

Little more than just a number on a page.

So what is this magic remedy we use?

Well, let me give you a few little clues.

It's applied at least weekly, always outdoors,

And no, we don't rub it into our pores

But regular doses give us a healthy glow

Anyone can see we've got a fairway to go,

Because we rarely flag, we haven't lost our grip

And since the surgery we're feeling quite hip.

We've still got the right strokes, the touch, the feel

And we're all simply oozing with sex appeal,

Because look at the impression we're still making,

With multiple male partners ours for the taking,

Provided, of course, that they've still got the strength,

Because when it comes to the men we like a bit of length.

Someone who can still give it his best shot

And show us exactly what he's got.

But before you all start having the vapours

And firing indignant letter off to the papers

The remedy I'm referring to is not X rated

(Sorry if your interest has now evaporated)

Because what I'm talking about is golf, of course,

An age-defying pastime we can all heartily endorse.

So if all your joints have started to creak

And you're beginning to feel way past your peak,

Forget about buying all those expensive lotions

Or guzzling any suspicious looking potions,

Because all you need is a bag full of sticks, dear,

And then you too can take this magic elixir!

Boosting your street cred

Golf has an image problem, it's fair to say

Amongst those poor misguided souls who don't play,

You know how it is, people think it's rather sad

Played by the old and boring and borderline mad.

We know of course that this isn't true

But how best to counteract this view?

Strangely enough, formats might tick that box

Designed as they are to wrong-foot and outfox,

Because none of them does what it says on the tin.

Our Skins have got nothing to do with skin

And say bisque bogey to those not in the golfing loop

And they may very well be put in mind of a soup

And would no doubt therefore find it expedient

To avoid a dish with such an unsavoury ingredient.

Our bogey pars also sound worryingly nasal

And you only have to do the briefest appraisal

To see that our waltzes require no dancing flair,

And our fourball better balls are actually played in a pair

And our stablefords aren't remotely horsey

And while our mixed foursomes may sound rather saucy

We're just swingers of the club, as far as I know.

(Though if you want to give the other kind of swinging a go,

Stroke play may be worth bearing in mind

Although best ball might be considered a little unkind.)

So as you can see, formats are designed to mislead

But this ambiguity could be just what we need

To sex up golf's rather stuffy reputation

All it requires is a little exaggeration.

So next time someone tells you golf isn't for go-getters

Just a load of boring old blokes in Pringle sweaters,

Ask them if they've ever taken part in a mixed foursome

Give them a nudge, say they must, they're truly awesome

OK so *we* know our foursomes are usually very tame

But what about people who've never played the game?

They might think we're getting up to God knows what

And we'll go from being stuffy to being steaming hot,

Particularly when we mention our inflatable Pro!

So why not sex it all up a bit? Go on, give it a go,

Then you can sit back and watch your street cred soar

And you won't be just a sad old golfer any more.

But beware! You might gain such widespread renown,

That you'll end up known as the oldest swinger in town!

Golf Rules OK!

Well, actually no, it's not really OK

Because another thing about this game we play,

(Yes, there's more, I'm afraid, the list expands)

Are the rules which no one really understands.

Oh, they'll tell you something with complete conviction

Which then turns out to be a load of old fiction.

So take what people say with a pinch of salt

But remember, it really isn't their fault.

Look at the rule book, you'll understand why

Enough to make a grown woman cry.

Page after page of incomprehensible guff,

I mean, who exactly is writing this stuff?

Some poor sod perhaps locked in a room at the R&A

And never allowed to see the light of day,

No wonder he/she/they have lost the wood for the trees

It's the only way to explain rules like these.

I mean, a little clarity's not much to ask

Is there anyone out there up to the task?

Apparently not so just have a care,

And if you're new to golf also be aware

That there's an additional complication

That defies all rational explanation.

Because there are the rules and also the spirit of the game

And the two things aren't necessarily the same.

If by this point, as I can only assume

You've all run screaming from the room

Or are sitting there tearing out your hair,

Please don't completely despair,

Because despite all its linguistic abuses

The rule book does still have its uses.

So if you have trouble getting off to sleep

There's no need to lie there counting sheep,

Just read a couple of rules every night

And believe me, you'll go out like a light!.

So why do we play golf?

So why do we play golf, that's what I want to know?

Why on earth do we keep on giving it a go?

When it's a game we can never really master

Taking us quickly from triumph to disaster.

You hit a decent shot and shout hooray!

But before you get too carried away

Just remember that the next shot you hit

Is likely to be complete and utter... rubbish

And if the golf itself isn't bad enough

You have to put up with all the other stuff,

The formats which seem designed to provoke

Some of them just completely beyond a joke,

I mean, the Bisque Bogey. Give us a break.

And mixed gruesomes? Oh for goodness sake!

And don't even get me started on the yellow ball competition

Definitely not for people of a nervous disposition.

And take one look at the rule book and all it's got to give

And you'll very soon lose the will to live.

So what's the point of trying to hit something small and spherical?

Well, there's friendship and laughter, although mainly hysterical

And a kind of Blitz spirit of, 'we're all in this together.'

So when you've finally reached the end of your tether

And say, 'That's it, golf. We're finished. I've had enough.'

Just remember there's someone else out there stuck in the rough,

Or about to take seven off the tee in a medal competition,

Because let's face it, we've all been in the same position,

Head full of weird swing thoughts and mounting dread,

But what we should do is focus on this one fact instead:

Even though we know full well what's in store

We also know we'll keep on coming back for more,

Through howling winter gales and thick autumn mists

Because basically we're just a bunch of masochists

Which is just as well, because it's a fairly safe bet,

That the game of golf hasn't finished with us yet!

And the answer is....(the correct answer that is)

At the risk of boring you, (don't worry, I'm nearly done)

I shall ask that question again, you know the one.

Why do we play golf? Why on earth do we keep on playing?

OK, so we're masochists, that goes without saying

But there's something else I've overlooked,

Another reason why we all stay hooked,

Because when we're finally at the end of our tether

Everything will suddenly just come together,

And we'll play a round where we can do no wrong

All our drives are straight and true and long

And our woods are Tigerish, our chipping top notch

And our putting is simply a joy to watch.

When rounds like this will happen there's no way of knowing

But the possibility they might, that's what keeps us going.

So that's why we play golf, for better or for worse.

There you have it, your answer, in a little book of verse.

All proceeds from the sale of this book will go to the Sunnybank Trust, a small charity entirely dependent on donations which helps people with learning disabilities lead the lives they choose through a range of support services, including a befriending scheme, advocacy support, and regular social activities.

Printed in Great Britain
by Amazon

14456678R00021